SUNSHINE
ELEMENTARY

Written by
Nina Saporta

Illustrations by
Amanda Gallant

Cover Art by
Chelsea Ekberg

Sunshine Elementary

Copyright © 2019 Nina Saporta

ISBN 978-1-7338859-0-4 (paperback)

Printed in the United States of America

Library of Congress Control Number: 2019949428

CPSIA Code: PRFRE0619A

For distribution, please contact Mascot Books:

620 Herndon Parkway, Suite 320, Herndon, VA 20170

info@mascotbooks.com   www.MascotBooks.com

For all other inquiries, please contact Kids Are Kind Publishing:

P.O. Box 1113, Belmar, NJ 07719

Hello@KidsAreKind.com   www.KidsAreKind.com

Educator and librarian resources available at:

www.KidsAreKind.com/Resources

Visit Sunshine Elementary Books online at

www.SunshineElementaryBooks.com

A Message from the Author

To all children, from every corner of the world,
I'm so proud of you for being exactly who you
are. You are kind, you are capable, you are a
wonderful friend, and an amazing engineer.
Always remember, you will never regret being
brave enough to act on your kindness
(it's where all the magic happens).

To my rays of sunshine:

Audrey, Oliver, and Sebastian

Contents

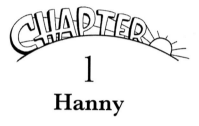

1

Hanny

Hanny sat on the floor lacing up her high-top sneakers with a blueberry waffle hanging out of her mouth.

"You're up early," Hanny's mom said as she walked into the kitchen with Hanny's two younger brothers trailing close behind. "How'd you sleep?" Hanny's mom took the waffle out of her daughter's mouth, put it on a plate, and handed it back to her.

"Sleep?! I was way too excited to sleep. Or maybe I was nervous. Or…curious? I don't know, but I didn't sleep at *all*." Hanny paused for a moment as her youngest brother, Sam, climbed into her lap.

"Although…" she began to recall, "I do remember juggling scoops of ice cream while jumping on a trampoline. Pretty sure I don't know how to juggle yet, so that must have been a dream. Okay, maybe I slept a little."

The image of Hanny's dream sent Sam and Julian into a fit of laughter.

It was hard to believe that it was really the first day of school. The summer had been filled with so many thoughts of this moment, and Hanny tried to picture them all: the kids, the teacher, what they'd be learning. There had been so many question marks dancing around in her head that it was hard *not* to think about it.

While Hanny couldn't help but wonder what the other kids would be like, she also tried to imagine what *she* would be like in school. Sometimes she felt really cool and old, like when her younger brothers asked her to play a song on the guitar or when she got to turn on the toaster oven by herself. But other times she felt sort of shy and embarrassed for what seemed like no reason at all.

"What do you think it's going to be like?" Hanny asked her mom, smiling through the butterflies that were welling up in her belly. She gently wiggled out from under Sam and sat on top of the counter by where her mom was standing.

"It's hard to say," Hanny's mom said as

she put down her coffee and looked at Hanny. "Everyone is different and will have their own personalities, so I would count on it being interesting! Plus, Sunshine Elementary is a brand-new school, meaning literally everyone will be the new kid today. I would guess that a lot of kids in your class are probably a little nervous right now."

That made Hanny think.

Jumping down from the counter, she took off running to her room before her mom could ask where she was going.

"Five more minutes, Hanny, and we'll be heading out the door!" her mom called after her.

"Five minutes," Hanny thought, "that's all I need."

Hanny reached into her Maker Cart that

4

stood next to her desk and pulled out some string, scissors, paper clips, and markers. The cart had been a birthday gift from her mom a few years earlier. It was loaded with all sorts of wheels, tools, clips, string, and anything else Hanny could possibly need to make new inventions or solve problems. She didn't have time to make anything right now, but she knew the supplies would come in handy at some point (they always did).

After zipping the materials into her backpack, she added a few more colorful bracelets to her already super-decorated wrist and headed toward the door. Catching a glimpse of herself in the mirror, she smiled her kindest smile.

"This is it," she whispered to herself.

2
Wilder

"*Goooooood* morning!" Wilder's parents sang in unison. Wilder rolled over, not because he minded that his parents were a little cheesy (although he did start to wonder if now might be a good time to get an alarm clock), but because he was *not* used to waking up this early.

Summer vacation had been one big Surf and Lounge Fest. He had gotten used to sleeping in, surfing through lunch with his big sister, Izzy, and relaxing by the fire pit deep into the evening.

"Okay, okay, I'm up," he promised as he shuffled his smiling parents out of the room. After a few sniff tests, Wilder slipped on his cleanest pair of board shorts and a hooded sweatshirt. He smoothed back his curly blond hair that went down just past his ears as one little curl popped back out, landing right in the middle of his forehead.

As Wilder stood cross-eyed staring at the curl, his sister, Izzy, opened the door and immediately burst out laughing at the sight of him. Wilder couldn't help but join her.

"I just came in to give you this," Izzy said as she handed him a braided string bracelet. Wilder took it in his hand and examined it. Izzy lifted up her arm to show that she had

the same one.

"It's a friendship bracelet," she said. "I thought it might help us today. You know, like, feel close even when we're not together. It's been so fun hanging out all summer, and I'm gonna miss you!"

Wilder smiled at his sister. "I'm gonna miss you too, Izzy."

"Breakfast is almost ready, kids!" they heard their dad shout from the kitchen.

"Be right down!" they both said at the exact same time.

"Jinx! Double jinx!" they shouted with a giggle.

While Izzy tied the bracelet around his wrist, Wilder looked out the window, trying to picture the building that would be his new school. He and his sister had skated past it for months, watching it grow bigger and looking more and more like a school as the summer came to an end. As relaxed as he was about starting school, the thought of not having his sister with him made him feel a little lonely.

"I'm excited that I get to drop you off on my way to middle school! And we'll probably even get home around the same time. We'll be back together before we know it," Izzy said.

Her brother smiled at the thought of them being back in this exact spot a few hours from now.

"Come on, kids, these pancakes aren't going to eat themselves!" they heard their dad call out from the kitchen.

They looked at each other with soft, bittersweet smiles.

"We'll be totally fine," Wilder said, trying

to sound convincing.

"Of course we will. It's gonna be great," Izzy said, giving his curly hair a rub before walking out of the room.

"Yeah," he said to no one in particular. "It's gonna be great." Looking down at the bracelet on his wrist, he took a deep breath and followed Izzy toward the kitchen.

3
Winnie

"Winnie?" Grammy Rose looked from one side of the room to the other, wondering where her granddaughter could possibly be. "*Winnie*?!"

"Balabalooa!!!" Winnie shouted as she jumped out from behind the closet door. Her grandma jumped so high that she nearly hit the ceiling.

"Winnie! You almost gave me a heart attack!" Grammy Rose laughed as she tumbled onto Winnie's bed to catch her breath. Even though sometimes the pranks drove her a little crazy, she loved this side of Winnie. There was never a dull moment living with such a funny, spirited kid.

Feeling pleased with herself, Winnie gave Grammy Rose her hand and helped her back onto her feet. "I'm *sooooo* excited for school to start! Is it time to leave yet?" Winnie asked.

"Honey…" Grammy Rose started, "I don't think you're *quite* ready to leave." She nodded toward the mirror.

Winnie looked in the mirror and noticed her rainbow-striped pajama pants and polka-dot shirt that read "Yes, I was born this awesome!" still on. She reached into her drawer, pulled out a tutu, and slipped it over her pajamas. She mixed a giant bow in with her soft black hair

and curtsied.

"*Now* I'm ready," she joked.

"Don't ever change!" Grammy Rose laughed as she started down the hall. "I'll see you downstairs in five."

It had been a bit of a quiet summer for Winnie. Her parents—both doctors—often traveled to take care of people in countries where there wasn't a lot of help available. Even though Winnie was used to them being away, and got to stay in her own home with her beloved Grammy Rose, she couldn't help but feel lonely at times. Being an only child can have its perks, but not having siblings to play with—*especially* when her parents were away—wasn't one of them. The thought of meeting new friends at school made her whole insides light up!

After Winnie got dressed, she walked into the kitchen where Grammy Rose was drinking her tea. "Come and see what I made for your first day of school," Grammy Rose said.

Winnie looked at the plate to find a face made out of breakfast food. There were blueberry eyes, a strawberry nose, a banana smile, and fluffy scrambled egg hair. Without skipping a beat, Winnie grabbed some kale out of the fridge and put it under the juicy red strawberry nose.

"Excuse me, Mrs. Breakfast Face, I think you need a tissue!" laughed Winnie.

"*Bon appetit*!" Grammy Rose replied as she lovingly rolled her eyes at her granddaughter before pointing out the kitchen clock. "Eat up, sweetie. It's just about that time…your new school awaits!"

Winnie felt a sudden rush of excitement, like the feeling of being at the top of a roller coaster.

"I am *so* ready for this! I just hope these classmates of mine have a good sense of humor!" Winnie said as she feasted on a giant bite through her wide-open smile.

4

Jonah

Jonah's eyes were closed as he breathed in slowly and deeply over his bowl of Starry Rice Puff cereal. Under the table, his toe tapped rapidly against the kitchen floor.

Although Jonah usually felt happy and calm, he had another side to him that was more nervous and anxious. Something that helped him relax when the more anxious side was winning was to *breaaaaaathe* in slowly until his chest was as big as it could get, and then letting it out like he was trying to blow out a birthday candle that was really far away.

Jonah's dad sat down next to him and rubbed his back. "Do you need anything, love?" he asked his son. Jonah continued his breathing with such deep concentration that he didn't answer.

"I know it can be scary to start a new school. Or anything new for that matter," his dad said. "You know what helps me in those situations?"

Jonah looked up for a moment to meet his dad's eyes.

"When I'm nervous about something," his dad started to laugh as he continued, "I like to picture in my mind what the absolute worst thing that could happen would be."

"Why are you laughing? That's not really funny, Dad," Jonah said with a slight smile.

"I swear! It worked when I was going through your adoption process—"

"Oh, this story again?" Jonah said under his breath.

"I was so nervous that things wouldn't go as planned, so I pictured what the worst thing that could happen would be," his dad shared, as if it was for the first time. "And I thought that the worst case would be that after all of that paperwork, and all of my excitement to have you as my son, I'd find out that, whoops! I accidentally applied to…"

"…adopt an elephant," they said at the same time.

"Oh, you heard that story already?" Jonah's dad asked with a smile.

"It's still funny, though," Jonah said lovingly.

"Okay, Jonah, now it's your turn," his dad encouraged. "What is the worst thing you can think of happening on your first day of school?"

Jonah sat back against his chair with a half-smile and looked up to the ceiling as he thought. "Okay, I think I have it," Jonah began. "I'm walking up the front steps at school and everyone in the whole school, like, the kids, their parents, the teachers, are all standing outside. Suddenly, I trip and fall flat on my face and everyone laughs at me," Jonah said with a worried look.

"Well that—" his dad started to say, but Jonah continued on.

"And that morning I somehow totally forgot to get dressed, so for whatever reason

I'm in nothing but my underwear."

"Yeah, I can see how—" his dad tried adding but, again, was interrupted by Jonah continuing the story.

"And for the rest of the school year, everyone sang, 'Underpants boy is falling down,' to the tune of 'London Bridge Is Falling Down.'" And with that, Jonah started to laugh. He couldn't help it; the image was so ridiculous, it had turned funny.

"Okay, now keep walking us through the story. What happens next?" his dad asked.

"Oh, uh…I guess I would be pretty upset for a while. Then, eventually everyone would probably forget about it and I'd be okay. Or maybe no one would really care and they'd just move on right after it happened. Or! Maybe someone would take the time to help me up and give me some of their clothes and we'd end up being best buds!" Jonah stared off with a smile, imagining the scene.

Jonah's dad looked at him contently as he sat back in his chair. He felt happy to have been able to relieve his son from some of the nervousness that he was feeling. It was a trick he himself had used for years whenever he was scared of something.

"Honestly, Dad, I kind of feel like I can handle anything now! No matter what comes my way today, I will be totally fine. *Even* if I fall in front of the whole school," Jonah laughed. He seemed to have a weight removed from his shoulders as the nervous feelings started to fall away. He turned his focus to his bowl of cereal. "Thanks, Dad," Jonah said right before taking a bite.

A few minutes later, to the tune of "London Bridge Is Falling Down," his dad sang, "It's time to go to school my son, school my son, school my son, it's time to go to school, and maybe fall in front of everyone." They both started laughing as they headed toward their bikes awaiting them outside the front door.

5
Welcome to
Sunshine Elementary

The sun shined bright, alone in a blue sky without a single cloud around. A warm breeze carried with it memories of summer, but the image of children with backpacks quickly refocused the occasion back to the first day of school. Kids walked in small parades from their neighboring homes, some dragging along pouting younger siblings who couldn't quite understand why they too weren't going to school.

Shiny yellow buses pulled up under the weeping willow trees that lined the entranceway to the school as students poured out onto the pavement. Cars of all colors and sizes parked along the freshly painted curb as parents and relatives gave long hugs and shared encouraging words. Through all of the commotion, a blanket of excitement covered the entire block. After all, it was the first day of school at Sunshine Elementary!

Wilder's skateboard wheels came to a sudden stop as he planted his foot firmly on the sidewalk in front of the school. Izzy rolled up right behind him, looking relaxed and cool as always. She gave her brother a hug before they broke out into their secret handshake. Their parents trailed behind them.

"I'm off to middle school now. Wish me luck! Oh, and feel free to invite any of your new friends out surfing with us anytime. Take care, little bro. Have a great first day!" Izzy smiled as she stepped back on her board and began skating down the road. With one last glance back, she held up her left arm showing their friendship bracelet. Wilder did the same. As Izzy continued skating, she looked smaller and smaller until she turned a corner and was gone.

Suddenly, Wilder's parents were standing right beside him. Side by side, they walked toward the front steps leading to two tall red doors.

Meanwhile, Hanny and Winnie both pulled

up to the front of the school at the same time. Hanny swung on her backpack and headed toward the sidewalk as Winnie waited for Grammy Rose to walk around the car. The two girls made eye contact and smiled, quietly wondering if they would be in the same class.

Just as Hanny was about to open her mouth to say hi, their stare was interrupted by a loud *CRASH*. They both turned their heads to see Jonah flying through the air. His bicycle had hit the curb as he was riding up to school and there he was, catapulted into the sky and about to land right on the pavement...no wait, the bushes...Grammy Rose...bushes! Jonah landed with a *crunch* head first into a bush, with only his legs sticking out of the top.

What had looked like bees buzzing around a hive only moments before turned into total stillness, as the crowd froze in its tracks with a look of shock on every face. Wilder had heard the sound of the bike crashing from inside the school foyer and ran straight back out to see what had happened.

While everyone stood as still as statues, Hanny, Winnie, and Wilder ran straight for Jonah. The three, never having met each other, looked with kindness and determination into one another's eyes as Hanny said, "On the count of three! One…two…three!" and out came a little leafy, but otherwise totally fine, Jonah.

"I'm okay!" Jonah shouted as he reassured the crowd with an awkward wave and a red face. When he made eye contact with his dad across the yard, they both started laughing and shaking their heads in

shock and disbelief. Then, as if someone had pushed the play button, the scene began to move again as students and their families continued toward the school entrance.

While pulling a leafy twig out of Jonah's helmet, Hanny introduced herself to their small group. "I'm Hanny. I'm really sorry that this happened to you…" Hanny stared at Jonah, realizing she didn't know his name.

"I'm Jonah," he said, smiling shyly as he unbuckled the helmet from his head.

"Jonah. I'm sorry this happened to you, *Jonah*. Though, I've got to hand it to you… you have really good aim when it comes to not landing on pavement. That was honestly, really impressive. And to be able to laugh about it! Again…impressed!" Hanny said.

"I'm pretty sure I would have landed *directly* on my face," Winnie laughed. "I'm Winnie by the way," she said with a big wave and flashy smile. "And extra points for not turning my grammy into a pancake!"

The three of them looked at Wilder. "Oh! Hey. I'm Wilder," he said, shifting his skateboard as he reached out to shake hands with his peers. He worried that shaking hands was a little formal, but he could hear Izzy's voice in his head reassuring him that as long as he was confident about it, no one would think it was weird.

"That was really cool of you guys to help me. I wasn't planning on starting my first day with such a grand entrance, but here I am! Whose class are you in?" Jonah asked.

All at once, the three of them answered, "Mr. Tenderheart." They looked at each other with a combination of surprise and joy.

When Jonah replied, "No way! Me too!" they suddenly realized that the faces they were staring at were the faces of their new friends.

6

The Classroom

The second floor classroom door had a hand-written "Welcome Friends!" sign hung above the standard plaque that had Mr. Tenderheart's name on it. One at a time, the new friends filed into the classroom and began to look around. The parents and grandparents waved one last loving goodbye from the door as they headed back down the hall.

The room felt fresh and airy, with sunlight

shining through the giant glass windows that overlooked the beautiful trees out front. Glossy wooden tables stood in perfect order, with three or four chairs tucked snuggly underneath each one. Pencils poked out of beautifully decorated cups on each table, erasers pink and pure standing nearby to help give a spelling error or math mistake a second chance. And in the corner stood an inviting library nook, with a line of bookshelves and comfortable pillows on the floor.

There were a few other kids already in the classroom when Hanny, Wilder, Winnie, and Jonah walked in. Hanny remembered what her mom had said that morning, about how nervous some people might feel on the first day of school. Even though Hanny herself had been pretty unsure, thinking about helping her

classmates through their nervousness made her feel really brave for some reason.

"Hey, everyone! I'm Hanny! What are your names?" she asked the kids who were already standing around the room.

Two boys quickly answered at once with a name that sounded like "Holdry," which caused them to burst into laughter. They tried it again, one at a time, which revealed that their names were actually Henry and Holden. They had similar voices and their faces seemed to move through the same expressions. As Winnie stared at them, trying to figure these two out, they said in unison, "We're twins."

Winnie pointed at them and snapped excitedly, saying, "Ohh!" as if a big mystery had just been solved. With the attention now turned toward Winnie, she introduced herself to the class with her usual enthusiasm. "I don't have a twin, but I have at *least* two different personalities!" she joked.

Suddenly, a small voice came from behind them. "Hi," the voice said as the group turned to find a petite girl with red hair and freckles. A blank face turned to a small smile as she said, "I'm Olive," through blushed cheeks.

Just as Jonah was about to introduce himself, another group of about twelve students funneled through the class door. Considering that there were now about twenty kids in the room, it was oddly quiet. They seemed to all be taking each other in, maybe picturing a day later in the school year when they'd all know each other so well. But for now, they were strangers. Each person was new and trying to find a balance between wanting to know the other kids in their class and also figuring out their own place in this new environment.

Some kids had smiles on their faces and made eye contact, while others looked nervously down at the floor. One boy even seemed angry and annoyed. Hanny tried to smile at him, but he broke eye contact and looked quickly out the window. Another girl looked like she was trying to hide behind the group of kids.

Wilder ran over to help one of the students whose wheelchair had gotten stuck on the side of the door. He liked the way it had been decorated with stickers and colorful paint.

"Thanks, man. I'm Coleman," the boy said.

"I'm Wilder!" Wilder said as he looked at Coleman's shirt to see a familiar band logo. "You like the Bouncing Souls too? I saw them last weekend with my sister, Izzy!"

"What!? No way! I was there too!" Coleman exclaimed as he started to sing, "We are the true believers," with Wilder joining in.

Suddenly, the class's attention shifted toward the hall as they heard a strong, warm voice wrapping around the corner. "Sorry, class! I had to grab something from the office…here I am!"

Everyone stared at the door, waiting to see what the person attached to the voice would be like. Finally, he caught up with his words and there he was, standing in the doorway: Mr. Tenderheart.

7

Mr. Tenderheart

Mr. Tenderheart wore a colorful, fitted sweater that had a soft white collar folded over the top. His skin was the color of warm caramel and his brown hair sat neatly on top of his head, brushed to one side with a distinct part. He stood smiling as he looked around the class, his eyes wrinkling up at the edges. There was an ease about him as he glided to the center of the room, students parting naturally as he passed them.

"Wow," he said, looking around the room with his hands clasped together and an open smile on his face. "Welcome, friends! Unless you're in the wrong class, I'm your teacher, Mr. Tenderheart. I have a feeling this is going to be an absolutely amazing year."

Many of the students gave smiles in return, but everyone remained silent.

"Go ahead and sit down anywhere that is comfortable for you. At a table, on a pillow, on the windowsill…this is *your* space," Mr. Tenderheart said. The students shuffled around the room selecting spots to settle into. Some picked whatever option was closest to them, while others were more selective as they wandered around the room for a moment making a decision.

"I'll start by sharing a little bit about myself," he said with a wide smile. "I've been teaching for thirty years! I have three kids of my own who are grown up now. I live right down the road, and I couldn't believe it when they decided to build this beautiful new school!"

Mr. Tenderheart surprised the class when he jumped onto his desk.

"I love to dance," he said as he tapped his feet and spun around. "I love to sing," he sang dramatically like an off-key opera singer. "Still working on that one though," he laughed as he hopped back to the floor. "And most of all," he paused, looking joyfully and sincerely into the eyes staring back at him, "I love to teach."

The students seemed to breathe out a collective sigh of relief as the nervousness

they had been carrying with them started to evaporate.

"This is going to be amazing," Hanny thought to herself.

CHAPTER
8
Who Are You?

"Okay, now the first order of business," Mr. Tenderheart said while picking up a clipboard from his desk. "Who are you?" he asked as he looked around the room. "I have a list of names here on my attendance sheet. When I call your name, I don't just want to know what your name is, I also want to know *who* you are. Try to think of a word you would use to describe yourself so we can get to know you better. And also please let us know if you have a nickname you'd rather we call you by."

He cleared his throat and began going down the list alphabetically as the students did their best to try to think of a word to describe themselves.

"Anne."

"I prefer Annie, please. I love doing art, so I'd say creative."

"Coleman."

"I'm gonna go with adventurous. And Coleman is fine."

"Hannah."

"It's actually Hanny. And I think I'm kind. No, loving…can I be both?"

Mr. Tenderheart laughed gently. "You can be anything you want to be, and those are two very wonderful things to be."

As Mr. Tenderheart started reading the next name on the list, Hanny quickly added, "Oh, I'm also an engineer!"

Her teacher smiled again, thanking Hanny for her enthusiasm. "I think I speak for the whole class when I say that we're looking forward to getting to know you better, Hanny."

Hanny looked down, smiling with a hint of embarrassment. She thought that trying to describe herself with just one word was way too hard; there were so many things that made her "Hanny." She wondered if everyone else felt the same way about themselves.

Mr. Tenderheart called the next name on the list. "Henry."

"Handsome," he said, resting his smiling face in his hands, causing the class to laugh.

Shaking his head through a breath of laughter, Mr. Tenderheart continued. "Holden."

Rolling his eyes at his twin brother, Holden responded, "I'm definitely the handsome one," causing everyone to laugh again. "Get it…it's funny because we're twins!"

When the class was quiet again, the list continued.

"Jonah."

"Um, I'm nice and sometimes sensitive?" he said with a little bit of a shaky voice. He wasn't sure why, but his feeling of anxiety came back when everyone was looking at him. He knew it would pass soon.

"Lee."

Lee let out a breathy sigh like he was annoyed and couldn't believe he had to spend time answering this question. "Awesome," he said with a tone of sarcasm.

Hanny and Winnie looked at each other with concerned faces.

"Okay, Awesome Lee, it is really great to meet you!" Mr. Tenderheart said without skipping a beat.

Continuing through more introductions, the class began getting a sense of who was who. Many of the students described them-selves as some variation of fun, funny, nice, creative, or brave. Others shared that they were curious, hardworking, or athletic. As Mr. Tenderheart neared the bottom of the list, he called a name that had no answer: "Vida."

Everyone looked around the room in silence.

"Vida?" he asked again.

Slowly, in the back corner of the room, a hand began to move into the air. In a beautiful accent, with a slow and quiet voice, Vida simply said, "New."

"Welcome," their teacher said gently.

The class refocused their attention back to Mr. Tenderheart as he read the last two names.

"Now we have Wilder."

"Yes, that's really my name," started Wilder

confidently. "I'm not sure if this describes who I am or what I want to be, but I'm going to go with cool."

"How could someone named Wilder *not* be cool?" Mr. Tenderheart agreed.

"And last up we have Winifred."

Winnie cleared her throat. "I have a gigantic, colossal request, guys. *Please* do not *ever* call me Winifred. That name is reserved for when I'm in a lot of trouble, and is usually accompanied by my—not one, but *two* middle names—Shauna Bernice." Winnie jokingly smacked her forehead. "If you want to be my friend, it's Winnie. And if you don't want to be my friend...it's still Winnie." The class responded with a short burst of laughter, admiring her confidence and feeling happy to have someone with such a funny personality in the group.

"Oh, and a word I would use to describe myself is…serious," Winnie said jokingly.

"*Riiiight*," Mr. Tenderheart laughed.

There was a lightness in the room by the end of the exercise, as students started to feel more comfortable coming out of their shells. The classmates felt less like strangers and everyone relaxed a little more deeply into their seats as they waited to find out what came next.

9

Kindness Matters

Mr. Tenderheart thanked the class for the eventful roll call as he walked to the opposite side of the room. Next to the library corner was a large round rug, which he called their Meeting Mat. He sat down on it and paused.

"By now, you must all be experts at rules," he said. "Following them, breaking them, hearing them, debating them. We grown-ups *looooove* having rules for kids. In fact, I have a few that I'll share with you a little later. But what I'm most interested in right now are the rules *you* want to set for the classroom. Remember, this is *your* space. What are your class rules? I'd like you to work together as a class on the Meeting Mat to come up with them. Feel free to grab some paper and pencils from the tables."

The students looked around at each other while chairs squeaked out from under them. They came together on the rug as Mr. Tenderheart scooted more into the background. Once everyone was seated, a few people started talking at the same time.

"Okay, friends," Wilder finally said, trying to get everyone's attention. "No one can be heard when we're all trying to talk at once. Maybe we can pick something to hold and only the person holding that thing can talk. At least that part would be figured out."

Olive slowly held up a pillow that was next to her in the library nook. The pillow had a colorful pom-pom fringe and the words "Kindness Matters" embroidered boldly onto it.

"Yes!" Winnie exclaimed. "The Talking Pillow. That's perfect, Olive!"

"Did we just make our first rule?" Jonah asked the group, his confidence starting to come back. "When we're having a meeting, only talk when you have the Talking Pillow?"

Hanny grabbed a piece of paper and wrote it down as Rule #1.

The students looked pleased. Olive, still holding the pillow, pointed to the words on it.

"Kindness matters," Hanny read aloud as Olive passed the pillow to her. "Rule #2. I love it. Actually, do you all think we should bump that up to #1?" The students nodded.

The pillow started weaving its way around the group as students gave suggestions, worked through ideas, and agreed on a list of rules.

By the end, Hanny had written down the
following:

OUR CLASS RULES

#1 Kindness matters.

#*2 Only talk during a meeting when you
have the talking pillow

#3 Clean up after yourself.

#4 Always tell the truth.

#5 Treat others the way you want
to be treated.

6 Don't eat other people's snacks
without asking.

#7 Respect others and yourself too!

"Well done, class," Mr. Tenderheart said as he inched his way back into the group. "These are not only great rules, but I loved the way you all communicated *how* to come up with them. I try to let other adults in on my little secret that kids are so beautifully competent and independent when given the space to be. You'll also see how much more you'll enjoy following rules that you had a say in."

Many of the students felt a sweeping wave of accomplishment and confidence wash over them as they watched Mr. Tenderheart hang the paper onto the wall with a thumbtack.

"Now I'm going to ask everyone to please find a seat at a table so we can get to the main event."

"What's the main event?" Jonah asked.

"Learning, of course!" Mr. Tenderheart said with excitement.

CHAPTER 10
It Only Takes One Person

It hardly felt like two hours had passed. The students had been so deeply engaged with Mr. Tenderheart's lessons and the fascinating discussions that followed, they barely noticed that their stomachs had started to growl.

"Oh my!" Mr. Tenderheart said, looking startled at the clock as if it had suddenly popped out of the wall. "I didn't realize the time! Why don't you all grab your lunches, enjoy your food, and then we'll head outside for some fresh air."

A few students jumped right up to retrieve their lunch boxes, while others took a moment to file the papers from the lesson into their folder before getting up. Within a minute or two, everyone was already a few carrot sticks or sandwich bites into lunch.

As Mr. Tenderheart walked casually around the classroom, he heard snippets of different conversations floating out from the tables.

"...and then Izzy—that's my sister— grabbed me by my arm and threw me back up onto my board just before the wave knocked me right into the rocks!" Wilder told Jonah, Hanny, and Winnie, his hands holding pretzel rods as he showed the motion of the wave in his story.

"…but what I really want to do one day is go swimming with sharks! No, really! There's this cage you can go in underwater so they can't even take a single bite out of you!" Coleman shared bravely with Olive, Holden, and Henry, who debated whether or not that sounded like a fun idea to them.

"…nope, I didn't do anything fun this summer," Lee said dismissively as he took a bite of his sloppy joe. The other students at the table weren't sure how to respond. Annie broke the silence by telling a story about her science camp.

Mr. Tenderheart finished circling the room as he heard Winnie starting to say, "…maybe, just maybe, when they build the new playground outside, they can build us a stage! I think if I practiced enough, I could be really good at performing. My dad always says you can do anything if you practice enough!" Winnie beamed with excitement as she talked with her new friends about ideas she had for the empty schoolyard.

While listening to Winnie, Hanny kept seeing Vida out of the corner of her eye. She was sitting alone at a table, looking down at her lunch. Every time Hanny started to look over, she quickly refocused back to Winnie before Vida made eye contact with her.

Seeing Vida sitting alone made Hanny feel uncomfortable and sad, but she wasn't sure what she should do about it. After all, Hanny thought, she was new today, too. Shouldn't she focus on the new friends she already met so they could get to know each other better?

Hanny felt torn, but she couldn't stop looking over at Vida.

Suddenly, Hanny remembered something her mom had told her when she was young, something that hadn't *really* made sense to her until this moment: "It only takes one person to make someone not alone." She remembered her mom putting a doll alone on the table and asking Hanny to pretend it was a real person who felt lonely and sad. Then she took another doll out of the basket and placed it next to the first one. "See?" her mom said. "Now he's not alone! It didn't take the whole pile…it only took *one* to make a difference."

It was clear what Hanny needed to do.

With a brave, deep breath, Hanny excused herself from the table, picked up her lunch, and walked over to Vida's table in the back corner. Vida looked shocked to see Hanny coming and sat perfectly still with her eyes wide open as Hanny approached.

"Can I sit with you?" Hanny asked Vida, feeling a little tense and wondering if she should have just stayed at the table with her friends.

Vida looked straight up at Hanny, who stood next to the table, frozen, holding her lunch box. Hanny could see such a deep sadness piercing through Vida's eyes, and the discomfort of it made her start to regret coming over. But then, Vida's face began to soften as her lips curled into a smile. Vida pushed a chair out, inviting Hanny to sit down. With a feeling of relief, Hanny put her lunch box next to Vida's and sat down.

The two girls talked through the whole rest

of the lunch period. Hanny learned that Vida had come to the United States as a refugee from Afghanistan. "My country so beautiful, but my family not safe there, so we move here. It so different," Vida explained.

Hanny had never met anyone like Vida before. She had such a different life story than her own, but somehow, when they were talking, Vida didn't seem much different than any of the other kids she had met that day. They both laughed when talking about how silly their younger brothers were, and how much they wished their parents would let them watch more TV. Hanny couldn't believe she almost didn't come over to Vida's table.

As Mr. Tenderheart announced that it was recess time, Vida put her hand on Hanny's arm as she was starting to get up. She looked her in the eyes and said sincerely, "Thank you, Hanny." Hanny smiled back as she reassured Vida, "It was my pleasure!" and went to put her lunch away.

Hanny enjoyed their time together just as much as Vida did, but what Hanny did not know was that she was the first friend Vida had made since moving to the United States. It only took one person to make a difference, to make Vida not alone, and Hanny was that person. Vida would never forget that moment for as long as she lived.

11
Buried Treasures

The class moved through the halls in one single-file line until they reached the tall back door. When they entered into the green courtyard, the warm, fresh air reintroduced itself. Even though their classroom had such nice, high windows that made them feel almost like they were in a treehouse, there was nothing like being outside.

With the school being brand new, there

wasn't a playground or any other type of play equipment set up yet. The students didn't seem to mind, as they immediately began exploring their new territory.

Hanny was looking down at the dirt that lay unexplored in between the patches of grass when she noticed something shiny. "Hey, everyone, look! There are crystals buried in the dirt!" she said as she dusted off a shiny green rock.

A crowd gathered in excitement to catch a glimpse of her discovery before quickly fanning out to look for more dirt patches. Some students just moved the dirt around a little with their shoes, feeling too shy to really get involved. Others ran around the yard trying to find the best spot to explore. There were even kids crawling around, knees in the dirt, digging up the buried treasures.

Winnie excitedly brought over a sparkling red crystal to show Hanny.

"Wow, it looks just like a ruby!" Hanny marveled. Jonah and Wilder looked over Hanny's shoulder to see it before sharing their own findings. Vida walked past them smiling and super focused, her shirt folded up at the bottom to create a pouch to carry her prized possessions.

Lee looked bored as he kicked the dirt, pretending not to care, although deep down all he wanted was to join his classmates. When no one was watching, he'd look down under his shoe to see if any crystals could be spotted. He didn't dare reach down to pick up a shiny gold stone that reflected like a disco ball in the sunlight.

"Hey, Lee! I think there might be a crystal under your shoe!" Winnie pointed out with excitement as she walked by.

Lee quickly pressed the crystal deep into the dirt. "No, there's not! And even if there was…who cares?" he said, his eyes turned away. He hadn't noticed that Winnie had been watching.

Winnie wasn't quite sure how to respond. Everyone else she'd met so far had either been friendly or just a little quiet and shy. Lee, on the other hand, was different. After a moment of feeling frozen, Winnie extended her hand with a few crystals resting on her flat palm. "Would you…like one of mine?" she offered.

"I said, I don't care," Lee whispered, his voice less convincing this time. His eyes went from looking across the yard to looking down

at the ground.

"Okay, Lee…well, let me know if you change your mind!" Winnie said, as friendly as possible, even through the awkwardness of the situation. Lee's eyes turned up to meet the back of Winnie's head as she started walking away to find her friends.

Lee wondered why someone would be so kind to him when most people in his life react by pushing him away. Could Winnie tell that he didn't mean what he said? Behind the deep feelings of pain and confusion that often tumbled around inside of him, a little flicker of hope and happiness started to grow. "Maybe school won't be so bad after all," he thought to himself. He turned his back to the scene so no one could see the subtle smile that popped up ever so quickly onto his face. Taking a seat alone in the grass, he leaned against the fence to quietly watch the activity going on around him.

Meanwhile, Hanny looked around the courtyard, feeling happy to see so many of her classmates coming together to uncover the crystals and share the joy of their discoveries. While scanning the yard, she noticed Olive trying to quickly wipe away tears that seemed to be melting down her cheeks. Not knowing what was wrong, Hanny immediately started running over to Olive, grabbing the attention of other friends along the way.

"I'm fine, I'm fine!" Olive said, trying to force a smile through the raindrops that kept stubbornly streaming down her face.

"Olive, what is it? What's wrong? You can tell us!" Wilder reassured Olive as she looked around at the kids who were gathering, many of whom were giving warm and encouraging smiles. They looked on curiously as the crowd continued to grow.

"I just…I…I…couldn't find any crystals. Everyone found beautiful crystals…and I *love* crystals and…and…I just feel sad because I looked so hard and I couldn't find one," Olive said quietly, looking down at the ground in embarrassment. She didn't like having so much attention on her.

Just then, Vida walked from the back of the group straight through the crowd until she was standing right at Olive's feet. She gently took Olive's hands, turned them up to form a small bowl, and handed her the crystals she had collected. Every last one of them. Vida smiled, turned around, and walked back out of the crowd. Olive stared wide-eyed into her hands without moving. She was overwhelmed with joy and disbelief.

A moment later, Coleman wheeled himself through the crowd, reached into his pocket to pull out three shiny crystals, and added them to the pile that Vida had placed in Olive's hands. Hanny was next—then Jonah, Annie, Wilder, Holden, and a handful of other kids who had been in the crowd watching what was happening.

Mr. Tenderheart walked into the circle holding a hat, which he placed upside down next to Olive like a basket. "It looks like you could use this," he said, smiling and looking around the group with pride and admiration. "Man, kids are kind," he said, nodding his head as he walked back toward the fence to keep an eye on the rest of the class.

Olive whispered, "Thank you," as she knelt down to pour her overflowing hands into the hat. A smile spread so wide across her face that it nearly reached her ears.

12
Three Little Eggs

"What's that?" Jonah asked as he pointed across the yard at a group that was gathering in the opposite corner. One of the students from his class was holding something, but he couldn't quite make out what it was.

When no one answered, Jonah started walking across the yard to see what was going on. Hanny, Winnie, and Wilder followed behind him, bringing their curiosity along.

"It must have fallen from the tree!" one girl

said as she pointed up at the branches that towered above them. While everyone else looked up, Jonah and his friends fixed their eyes on what it was that was causing all the excitement. In their classmate's hands was a bird's nest made out of twigs. Inside the nest were three blue eggs.

"It's amazing none of them cracked on the way down!" one boy said.

"The nest must have acted like a pillow," Jonah added.

"So…how do we get it back up?" Hanny asked.

The entire group turned at once and looked at Hanny as though she had just suggested that they go on a trip to the moon.

"*What*?" Hanny asked with a smile.

"We can't do that! It's all the way up there!"

Henry said, as if Hanny was being ridiculous.

"We can do anything," Hanny reassured the group. "We just have to figure it out."

This made Henry laugh and start walking away, thinking there must be something more fun to do than watch the group attempt an impossible task. But Hanny's three new friends and a few other kids from their class kept a circle around the nest that held the three delicate eggs.

"So what are you thinking, Hanny?" Winnie asked as she looked to her friend with encouragement.

Hanny paused for a moment, looking around at the group who waited eagerly for a response. To their surprise, she asked, "What are *you* all thinking?"

Everyone silently looked around at one

another. When they realized that no one had an immediate answer, they started looking up at the tree, down at the grass, and searching their heads for a possible solution to the problem.

Jonah noticed something in the corner of the yard. "Maybe...oh, nevermind," Jonah said, feeling self-conscious.

"Hey, Jonah?" Hanny said gently. "I once read that when it comes to engineering, there is no such thing as a bad idea. And I really liked that because almost every time I try to engineer something, I fail a few times first. There's no pressure for us to get it right the first time around. Why don't you give it a shot?"

"Okay," Jonah said, feeling more confident. "Maybe...we...could *throw* it back up?"

"Interesting idea! Are you thinking that we,

just, like, throw the nest up at the tree? Or…"
Hanny asked, trying to fully understand what
Jonah had in mind.

"Well, I saw this ball over here," Jonah
said, going over to the corner of the yard and
picking up a grapefruit-sized rubber ball. "I
was thinking that maybe we could attach
the nest to the ball, and then throw it up to
the branch!"

"Let's try it! We can start by making a prototype, which is basically a fake version of it
to practice with first, just in case," Hanny said.

"Yeah, that sounds like a really smart idea,"
Jonah replied. "We're just getting warmed up."

Winnie bent down to gather some leaves
and branches, bunching them together to form
a makeshift nest. "I guess we never know
what's possible until we try! Here's a nest for

our prototype."

"How are you thinking of attaching it to the ball, Jonah?" Hanny asked.

Jonah shrugged his shoulders as he looked around the group for a suggestion.

Wilder had been chewing a piece of gum since after lunch. He took the sticky wad out of his mouth and held it out to Jonah.

With a somewhat hesitant and grossed-out face, Jonah took the gum. "*Thhhhanks*," he said with a smile, as he stuck the gum between the ball and the bunch of sticks.

"Okay! Let's do this!" Winnie said with excitement.

Jonah stood with the prototype in his hands. He felt pretty relieved that he wasn't experimenting with the real nest. Still, he hoped it would work. He took a step back.

Just as Jonah was about to throw the nest, Wilder shouted, "Hold it!" as he bent down to collect three small rocks from the ground. "We almost forgot our eggs!" He placed them into their practice nest as Jonah nodded.

"You can do it," Hanny whispered. They all looked on with anticipation as Jonah got ready to throw.

As he quickly launched the ball into the air, the sticks, rocks, and leaves immediately separated from the ball and spread out like fireworks, floating back to the ground. The ball flew high into the sky, over the fence, and was gone.

Jonah broke the intense silence when he started laughing. The group joined in. "Not even close!" Jonah said through his laughter.

Wilder saw that his gum had landed back on the ground. He picked it up, blew some of the dirt off of it, and put it back in his mouth. "Still good!" he announced, to his friends' amusement.

"Oh, yum!" Winnie joked. "Okay friends, we had our first successful failure! What else have we got?"

Hanny looked up at the tree as she

scratched her chin in deep thought. She looked around the yard and behind the tree before checking her pants pockets. She examined their contents, which included some lint and a paper clip.

"There's got to be some way..." Hanny started to think aloud while rubbing the paper clip between her fingers. "I've got it! I'll be right back!" she yelled into the air, hoping the breeze would carry the message to her friends as she took off running toward the door. By the time she reached her teacher, her plan was as clear as the sky above her. "Mr. Tenderheart, could I please run in and grab something from my backpack?"

"Sure, Hanny, but please come straight back out," he replied as he held the door open for her.

CHAPTER

13

There Are Many Ways to Solve a Problem

A few minutes later, Hanny was running back across the courtyard with her hands full of the items from her Maker Cart. She knelt down in the middle of the circle where her friends and classmates had been waiting. As she opened her hands toward the ground, two markers, a spindle of string, a pair of scissors, and three paper clips tumbled gently into the grass.

Hanny stood back, the confidence beaming out of her, as she assessed her plan one more time. The rest of the kids in the group just looked at her, having no idea what would happen next.

"What are you thinking, Hanny?" Wilder asked, staring up at the tree branch.

Hanny pointed up at the tree. "I think that big thick branch right there looks like a stable spot to put the nest. We can use the branch *above* it to make a pulley. We just need to get the other end of the string over that high branch and back down to us. Then when we pull it, it'll raise the end with the nest until it's all the way up to the branch!"

"We just have to make sure the nest is super secure to the string. I'm not sure how sticky—or reliable—Wilder's gum is at this point," Winnie said, looking at Wilder with a wink.

"I think I have just the tools to do it," Hanny replied. Slowly and carefully, Hanny took the nest in her hands and placed it softly onto the grass. She straightened out one end of each of the paper clips and hooked them carefully into the edges of the nest. Pulling slightly to make sure they were all securely attached to the bundle of woven twigs, she bent the paper clips back into a loop shape so that they wouldn't slip out. The nest now had three wire loops attached to it.

Winnie knelt down and gave the loops a gentle tug to double check that they were secure. "So far, so good!" she said to Hanny with a thumbs-up.

Hanny remained focused as she took the string and unraveled it until it was a pile on the ground. She cut three pieces of string, about six inches long each, and tied them to the paper clip loops. Then she tied the long pile of string to the ends of the three shorter strands. Hanny's friends watched silently, totally fascinated.

"Wow…this could really work!" Jonah said.

Stepping back to stare at the tree branch, Hanny looked up, then back down at the nest and string, then back up again.

"Now, do we have any ideas of how to get the string up that high?" Hanny asked her friends.

"Maybe we can climb the tree and when we get a little higher up, throw the string over the branch?" Winnie suggested.

"I totally support anything you want to try!" Hanny said.

Winnie jumped up, wrapping her arms and

legs around the tree. There she clung, frozen about a foot off the ground, unable to move any higher. Laughing at herself, she asked, "Am I almost there guys?" before hopping back down to join her giggling friends. "I swear, I'm usually a pretty good tree climber!" Winnie insisted. "I've been practicing since I was little. But this is a really thick tree! And with no low branches to grab onto, I think we're going to need a new plan to get up *that* high."

"If only we could find a way to make the other end of the string a little heavier, maybe then we could throw it over the tree," Wilder thought aloud.

"Yes! I think you're onto something, Wilder," Hanny said with excitement. Getting to problem solve with friends was just about

Hanny's favorite thing in the world to do. There are so many different ways to solve a problem—that was what Hanny loved most about engineering and her Maker Cart. It was always fun to hear what other people would come up with.

"What could we use?" Winnie asked as everyone in the group started to look around.

"There's not much around here. Another ball or even a stick would be great, but I don't see a single one of those things," Jonah said as he looked around the other side of the tree.

Hanny bent down into the grass to where she had originally placed her Maker Cart supplies. She picked up the marker and held it out to Jonah.

"This should do," Jonah said as he knelt down and tied the end of the string tightly around the marker. He handed the marker with the string back to Hanny. "You've got this," he said, smiling at his friend.

Hanny took a step back. She held her gaze up at the branch, then double-checked that the string wasn't tangled. She looked down once more at the nest and then back up at the tree. Her arm went back behind her head rapidly, with the marker gripped firmly in her hand. Suddenly, Hanny snapped her arm forward, releasing the marker midair.

The marker flew through the air with the string soaring behind it. Everyone held their breath as they watched the marker go higher and higher, the distance between the marker and the branch getting smaller by the second. With a perfect arc, the marker floated right over the upper branch and started its journey back toward the ground.

"You did it!" everyone cheered, as the marker landed safely back on the grass.

Hanny smiled as she picked the marker back up. With intense concentration, she pulled gently on the string until the nest slowly began rising into the air.

"It's really working!" Winnie whispered excitedly.

Inch by inch, the nest rose until it was high in the air, dangling above the branch that Hanny had selected as the resting place for the three eggs. She lowered the nest slowly and carefully, making sure it would land perfectly balanced on the limb. There were only a few inches left to go. Everyone held their breath.

Suddenly, one of the paper clips slipped out and the nest began to tip. The crowd

gasped, but Hanny remained calm. Before any of the eggs could roll out, Hanny quickly lowered the nest onto the branch. The eggs were safe! The crowd cheered for Hanny.

"It was all of us! We did it together." Hanny smiled proudly. The group beamed with relief as the crowd clapped and shared a round of high fives.

"What about this long extra string that's dangling?" Wilder asked.

"I've got this," Winnie said. She threw the marker a few more times around the branch so that the string was secure and much shorter. Then, she put the scissors into her back pocket and asked her friends to give her a boost higher up onto the tree. As she wrapped her arms and legs around the tree once more, she worked with all her might to reach out and grab the marker that was dangling in the air overhead. Before hopping back down, she cut the string and the marker came tumbling to the ground.

"That was amazing, Winnie! I loved the way you didn't give up, even when it got hard," Hanny said. "Plus, now the bird can use the extra string for its nest!"

"I just can't believe we did it!" Jonah said.

"I can!" replied Hanny, smiling.

Mr. Tenderheart and a few other class-mates had come over from around the yard to see what the group had accomplished. As they pointed and smiled at the nest sitting safely on the tree branch, a bird suddenly swooped in, perching happily on the eggs. The crowd cheered.

"I can't imagine a more magical way to end

recess," Mr. Tenderheart said.

Hanny slipped the markers and scissors back into her pocket as the group followed Mr. Tenderheart's request to line up to go back inside.

While the students walked back into their new school building, they noticed something shining on the ground. There, pressed into the dirt outside of the door, was a heart-shaped stepping stone made out of colorful crystals. As they all commented on how mysterious and beautiful it was, Olive kept her eyes to the ground, but she couldn't hide her smile.

CHAPTER
14
And Then I Jumped

"What are you doing after school today?" Jonah asked Wilder as they walked down the long hall back toward their classroom, their shoes squeaking under them on the glossy floors. A few of the students twisted their feet as they walked, trying to amplify the chorus of high-pitched *eeks*.

"Um...probably gonna relax then catch some waves with Izzy after dinner," Wilder said with a casual smile.

"Can you believe that I've lived by the beach for almost two years now and I still haven't surfed?" Jonah confessed to Wilder. "When I found out my dad and I were moving here for his new job, the only part I was excited about was getting to live by the beach so I could learn to surf. There was this taco restaurant near our old house that would play these amazing surf videos. I remember watching them from the time I was a kid and wishing that could be me!"

"That must have been hard to move somewhere new, but I can't imagine a better place to live! I was born here, so I don't even know what it's like to not be near—or in—the ocean. And surfing is just the greatest feeling in the world! I literally grew up on a surfboard. I have pictures of me as a baby riding on the end of my dad's longboard."

Jonah lit up as he heard Wilder describe his surfing experiences.

Wilder continued, "I get that you didn't grow up by the beach, but you're here now! If you've wanted to surf so much…why on earth haven't you?"

"Honestly? Do you want to know the real reason?" Jonah asked Wilder as they both stopped walking to look at each other. Wilder stood in suspense waiting to hear what Jonah was going to say.

"I…" Jonah looked seriously at Wilder. "I… have no idea," he said as his face changed to a smile. "I guess I just haven't had the chance to try it!" Jonah shrugged.

Hanny, catching the last part of their

conversation, put her arm around Jonah as they walked. "Jonah! If you want to do something, you have to just *do it*," Hanny encouraged her friend. "You can't wait for surfing to come *to you*!"

"Well, technically, the waves do kind of come to you," Winnie said, nudging Hanny with a smile. "But yeah, I'm sure you'd be awesome, Jonah!" Winnie added. "With all of your experience falling into bushes, just imagine how much softer water will feel!" she giggled. Jonah pretended to give Winnie an upset look, but he quickly joined in on the good-natured laugh.

"Okay, I'm going to do it. I'm going to try surfing!" Jonah said decidedly.

"Awesome! Let's all meet at six o'clock. South Bonnie Beach. I'll bring my extra board,"

Wilder said.

"Wait, like, today? Um, that sounds so awesome, but I, uh, I think I need to help my dad with something after school," Jonah fumbled, with a look of nervousness. In that moment, it became clear to both Jonah and his friends that the only thing that was stopping him from surfing was his own fear. The conversation ended abruptly as they wound back through the door of their classroom.

Mr. Tenderheart walked in behind them, having heard their whole conversation. He walked up to the front of the class and leaned back against his desk as the students settled back into their seats.

A velvety breeze slipped through the screened windows as the students held their gaze on Mr. Tenderheart, who stood in silence with his eyes closed. Just as awkwardness and curiosity started to peek their heads into the room, Mr. Tenderheart opened his mouth to speak. He kept his eyes closed as the students listened with total concentration to what he was about to say.

"I…was always terrified, *terrified*, of the water. I did not know how to swim because I refused to put as much as a toe anywhere that wasn't a bathtub. When I was a child, all of my friends would spend their summers swimming in our local lake. They would splash and make up games to play in the water. They laughed with such joy—the kind of joy that fills your whole body up. As they enjoyed playing and cooling off in the water, I simply sat, alone and hot, in the grass or up in a tree, just watching. I myself didn't experience it. I watched other people experience it, but I did not. Because I was scared. When I got older, my friends *still* enjoyed the water. And I *still* watched from afar."

"*Twenty-eight years* into my life of being afraid of water, I was on vacation in Greece and I found myself on this beautiful, gigantic sailboat. Picture the most captivating of all of the crystals you found today. Imagine one that was a bright, shimmering blue that you could see right through as you held it up to the sky. That's what this water looked like. Beauty I've never seen before, just sparkling like a blue diamond, begging me to be a part of it. I stood on the edge of the sailboat in my life jacket, holding onto the thick, rough rope that stretched into the sky. The wind was soft and the water calm as we anchored into stillness. As I looked down at the water—the same water that had been calling my name since I was a child—I pictured all of the times in my life that I had wanted so much to swim but had been too scared. All of those experiences that I watched pass me by that I never got to live. That I would never get back." Mr. Tenderheart paused.

"And then I jumped."

The students sat up in their seats, surprised at the turn that their teacher's story had just taken. They were completely focused on every word.

"And that jump changed my life. It *gave* me life. As I lay on my back, wet and weightless, floating in the sea with the water wrapped around me, I felt the embrace of all of life's possibilities. It just felt *so good* to finally be in that water. I made a promise to myself in

that very moment, that I would never miss out on another opportunity to experience life. I would say *'yes'* instead of *'no,'* and *'can'* instead of *'can't.'"*

Mr. Tenderheart started walking around the room, staring at the students' eyes as he continued. "The thing is, class, there will always be things that scare us, right? But we can't let that be the reason not to do something. There is just so much joy to be felt, so much learning to do, so much to give to others, and so many experiences right at our feet at any given moment. We just have to go out and live them. Since that moment, I have traveled to all seven continents, taken up dance lessons, volunteered more times than I can count, and I've gotten to teach my kids by example what it looks like to live. I hope to do the same for you as your teacher," Mr. Tenderheart said as he returned to the front of the room.

"Oh, and the ending of that story of me jumping off of the sailboat? It took the entire boat crew to fish me out of the water with this long pole because I couldn't climb back up the side," Mr. Tenderheart said as he and the class burst out laughing. "It was like something out of a movie! There I was, gracefully conquering my biggest fear in this beautiful moment, followed by me having to yell to my husband, 'Help! How do I get back on the boat?!'" They laughed together as a class once more.

"So to those of you who have ever wanted to try something new or explore an idea but felt too scared, I encourage you to make a promise to yourself, right here and now, to push past that fear and live. Always choose to live," Mr. Tenderheart concluded with a smile.

"Okay! So, moving on, is anyone interested in what happens beneath the Earth's surface when a volcano is erupting?" Mr. Tenderheart asked as he got out his science book.

Jonah suddenly leaned over to Wilder and whispered, "Six o'clock. South Bonnie Beach."

Wilder nodded with an impressed smile as he looked to Hanny and Winnie. "Six o'clock."

CHAPTER
15
Peak and Pit

Time flew as the class erupted a volcano with baking soda and vinegar, played a fun math game, and read a few chapters of a book together. Before they knew it, it was almost time to go home.

"Class, I have to say, this was a truly outstanding first day! Wouldn't you agree?" Mr. Tenderheart asked with a big smile.

Most of the students nodded and smiled,

and a few answered "Yes!" enthusiastically.

"This is only the beginning," their teacher continued. "I cannot wait to get to know you better, for you to get to know each other better, and most of all, for you to know *yourselves* better! It's going to be an amazing journey, and I hope you'll learn a lot along the way.

"Now, before class is dismissed, I'd like to end each day with everyone reflecting on your Peaks and Pits. The Peak is the best part of your day. The Pit is the lowest point, which is often our greatest learning experience. I'll call on three people each day to share their Peak and Pit with the class."

Mr. Tenderheart paused as the class sat in silence, thinking through all of the events of their very long and eventful first day of school. Outside of the closed door, parents began peeking through the window, trying to catch a glimpse of what was going on inside.

Mr. Tenderheart remained focused on the class as he called out, "Henry. Olive. Hanny. We would love it if you would be willing to share your Peaks and Pits with us."

Henry started. "Well…outside at recess, I saw across the yard how a group of kids worked together to put a bird's nest back into a tree using *string*! I'd never seen anything like it! It was so cool and I couldn't believe they actually did it. Or that they even thought to *try* to do it! So, getting to see that was my Peak."

Henry then looked down at his hands as he continued talking. "And my Pit was that…I had a chance to be a part of it. And I wasn't. I walked away because I didn't think something like that was possible. I didn't even try. I really regret that," Henry said, feeling a little ashamed.

"Aw, Henry," Hanny started to respond from across the room, "I promise there will be plenty more chances to engineer together!" Henry's somber face lightened up into a smile.

"I wasn't kidding about how much we learn from our Pits!" Mr. Tenderheart added.

"That's for sure," Henry said, as he leaned back into his chair.

"Olive? Would you mind sharing *your* Peak and Pit?" Mr. Tenderheart inquired.

Olive was hoping that maybe he had forgotten that she was chosen to speak in front of the whole class, but she pushed herself to answer confidently. "I was given a really beautiful gift today from some new friends," Olive said, and then paused. "But that wasn't my Peak."

"No? Hm," Mr. Tenderheart replied, looking confused.

"My Peak was getting to give a gift back to my new friends," Olive said with a smile as she looked around the room at her classmates. In this moment, the class realized it was Olive who made the heart-shaped stepping stone outside. The room buzzed with excitement and chatter for a moment before Olive continued.

"And I think my Pit was when I couldn't find any crystals. But I don't care about that now."

Hanny sat up straight in her chair as she got ready for her turn to answer. By now most of the parents and grandparents were at the door waiting to pick up their kids from their first day of school.

Hanny cleared her throat. "Hey…okay…if it's all right, I'd like to start with my Pit. My Pit was before I came to school this morning. I had honestly been kind of nervous about the first day of school. Like, pretty much on and off for the whole summer. I didn't know if you would all be nice or not, or if we'd have a teacher that didn't like kids or something crazy. Sometimes not knowing is the scariest part!" Hanny said, as she looked around the room, a few kids nodding in agreement.

"And my Peak…oh man…I had so many Peaks today! For one, we seem to have a really cool teacher."

This made Mr. Tenderheart smile warmly and mouth the words "thank you" to Hanny.

"We got to make this classroom our own, which made me really happy. I got to feel proud of myself for helping to engineer a solution to a problem. And most of all, I got to meet all of you." Hanny smiled as she looked around the room at the faces that were starting to feel more familiar. Hanny really meant this. She felt like everyone in the class had something different and wonderful to add, just as her mom had said.

"Thank you, Henry, Olive, and Hanny for sharing. I love the opportunity to get a glimpse into what this experience is like for each of you. And thank you everyone for a magical first day. What a remarkable year this is going to be! Enjoy the rest of your day, and I'll see you in the morning," Mr. Tenderheart said before moving toward the door and opening it to a crowd of eager loved ones.

The students said goodbye to one another

as they gathered their belongings and made their way toward the familiar faces of their families. Coleman and Wilder gave each other a high five as Hanny and Vida shared one last smile and wave. Mr. Tenderheart shook each student's hand as they left the classroom, encouraging them to make eye contact with him as they did so.

16
This is Only the Beginning

Like small streams joining to form a mighty river, the students filed out of their classrooms and into the main hallways, moving as one out of the school. Hanny, Wilder, Winnie, and Jonah were still side by side by the time they got to the sidewalk.

"I'm really glad to have met you guys," Hanny said to her friends.

"Me too!" Winnie blurted out excitedly.

"I'll see you all at the beach," Wilder said as he patted Jonah on the back.

Jonah smiled excitedly. "Six o'clock! I'll be there," he promised.

They each felt a sense of confidence as they parted ways, a lightness and happiness that came from getting to the other side of something new that some of them had been afraid of. There was so much to tell about their first day—so many stories and events—that they could hardly wait to share them.

As the friends walked off with their families, swirls of questions like, "So, how was your first day of school?" began to wrap around them in a warm, familiar embrace. The friends glanced back once more to exchange a smile, a wave, or one last "See you later!" before melting back into the comfortable routine of family.

The sun hung low in the still-blue sky as Hanny's feet stepped softly on the warm pavement on the way to the car. She paused for a moment before opening the door, staring back at her new school building. She closed her eyes, turned her face up to the warm sun, and exhaled the biggest smile. "This is only the beginning," she whispered to herself as she pulled the handle of the car door.

As Hanny buckled herself in, her mom twisted around in her seat to make eye contact with her daughter. It took all of her mom's strength not to pour out a million questions at once; she was so eager to hear how the day had gone. Finally, Hanny looked up at her and simply smiled. The smile said everything. The first day had been a success. Her mom nodded, smiling back with joy and relief into the rearview mirror. Hanny looked to her younger brothers, whose feet dangled happily in their car seats as she rattled off stories about her first day at school.

"More bird!" Sam begged when Hanny finished the story about the nest.

"No, crystals!" Julian insisted.

"I really liked the one where you were the reason Vida was not alone," her mom said with a wink.

"There will be more stories tomorrow. Promise." Hanny smiled as she stuck her arm out of the window to create a wave against the wind with her hand.

A few blocks over, Wilder skated down the street toward his house with his parents trailing farther and farther behind. He felt happy that the day had been so amazing, and all he wanted now was to be reunited with Izzy. As he skated rapidly toward home, he heard a familiar voice call out from behind him, "Hey! When did you get so fast?"

Wilder quickly turned his head just as Izzy was pulling up. He practically dove off his board to give her a hug.

"How great was it?!" Izzy sang to her brother, excited to hear about his day.

"Oh, Iz, it was awesome," Wilder started to share as they walked side by side with their boards under their arms. "I have so much to tell you! I made some really great friends, and we engineered a pulley to get a bird's nest back into the tree, and we got to make our *own* classroom rules, and there are *crystals* in the ground, and our teacher is super nice, and can you believe he was too scared to go swimming until he was a grown-up? Oh, and speaking of swimming, my friends are coming over at six to go surfing with us!" Wilder exhaled as Izzy tried to take in all of her brother's excitement.

"That all sounds *incredible*! I can't wait to meet them!" Izzy said.

"How was your first day of middle school?" Wilder asked.

"*Great*. You have so much to look forward to!" she replied.

"I think I'd be happy staying at Sunshine Elementary forever," Wilder said.

Izzy smiled. "I'm so glad to hear that."

Wilder and Izzy looked up as a passing car gave them a friendly beep, with an arm waving enthusiastically from the window.

Inside the car, Winnie exclaimed to

Grammy Rose, "That must be Wilder's sister,
Izzy! Do you mind if I go to the beach with
them after dinner? Hanny and Jonah will be
there, too. Oh I would be so happy if I didn't
have to wait all the way until tomorrow to be
back with my new friends!"

"Yes, dear, you can go. Of course you can
go. I can't believe you have plans already! It
sounds like you couldn't have dreamed up a

better first day of school!" Grammy Rose said as she looked at Winnie's excited face in the rearview mirror.

"It was better than a dream," Winnie said. She leaned her head out the window and shouted, "This is only the beginning!" followed by a giant, "Woohoo!" that echoed throughout the neighborhood.

Lee turned his head at the sound of Winnie's voice in the distance, faint but recognizable. He threw his backpack onto the seat as he climbed into the back of his stepmom's car.

"So…how was it?" she asked.

Just then, Lee noticed that the zipper on the small pouch of his backpack was undone. As he leaned over to zip it back up, something caught his eye—something shiny. Reaching into his bag, he felt the roughness of the jagged stone. Without hesitation, he pulled it out to find the golden crystal that he had secretly admired at recess, shining like a disco ball as he held it up. He squeezed it tightly in his hand, looking out the window with a smile.

"Fine," he finally replied to his stepmom. "My day was fine."

CHAPTER

17

As the Sun Set

"You're sure you're up for this?" Jonah's dad asked as they cleaned up their dinner plates.

"Dad, I don't want to just sit back and watch other people have life experiences and have none of my own. I can't let fear get in my way!" Jonah said triumphantly.

Jonah's dad took a step back and stared at his son.

"That was deep," his dad said, shocked

and impressed. "What are they teaching you at this school?"

Jonah laughed. "A lot," he assured his dad.

"Yeah, I'd say so!" his dad agreed. "So, surfing, huh? Sounds like it'll be fun! We *have* always wanted to try surfing."

"*We?* Um...Dad?" Jonah started. "I was kind of hoping to just go with my friends tonight. It's not that I don't want to hang out with you—"

"I get it. Friends are important at your age. At any age, really. Why don't you teach me what you learned over the weekend. We can rent boards down at Melly's Surf Shack."

"Sounds great, Dad. Thanks a lot for understanding," Jonah said.

"Oh, one thing...I *am* going to lifeguard from a distance though. Deal?" his dad asked.

"Deal," Jonah replied as he skipped to the door.

Wilder and Izzy were already in the ocean when they saw Winnie and Hanny heading across the warm, speckled sand to the water's edge. They greeted each other from a distance as Wilder popped up to catch a wave back toward the shore. His friends cheered for him as he coasted effortlessly under the crest.

Jonah and his dad appeared over the top of the dune a moment later. His dad waved from a distance, perched up high, while Jonah ran toward his friends.

"Hi, Jonah's dad!" The friends waved back.

"Jonah! You're really doing this!" Hanny said with total excitement as Wilder helped Jonah attach a velcro strap to his ankle.

"You're going to fall. Just embrace it. This

leash will make sure your board is never far when you do. Just get back up and try again. Eventually, you'll look around and realize you are standing on a moving wave, in the ocean, and it's the coolest feeling *ever*," Wilder said.

Just then, they all looked up as Izzy surfed the perfect wave to shore. She ran out toward the four friends with her surfboard under her arm.

"So great to meet you all! I'm Izzy! You must be Jonah, Winnie, and Hanny." They all smiled and greeted one another.

"I brought an extra board in case you want to surf, too," she said to Hanny and Winnie as she motioned toward a waxed up turquoise surfboard on the sand. Then she handed her board to Winnie. "You can use mine. I'm going to head back to do some homework. Have so much fun!"

Hanny and Winnie looked at each other excitedly as they knelt in the sand to attach the leashes to their ankles. When they were ready, they met their friends right on the edge of where the ocean meets the sand.

Jonah, Hanny, Winnie, and Wilder stood side by side, boards under their arms, staring out into the rhythmic ocean. No one said anything and nobody moved. Though they were all together, they were each in their own world, reflecting.

Jonah's mind was back in the restaurant watching the surf videos as a child. He thought through all of the times he had daydreamed about living this exact moment and how inspired he had felt in class to have this experience, even through his fear. His head

was held high as he awaited the opportunity to show himself—and his dad, from up on that dune—how brave he was.

Hanny's mind wandered to Vida's family as she tried to imagine what it must have been like for them to leave their home. She felt overwhelmingly lucky that she and her brothers happened to be born in a country at peace. That was all that set her and Vida apart. As she watched the waves break at her feet, she made a promise to herself to find more ways to help people who weren't as lucky as she was.

Wilder smiled at the feeling of having three new friends beside him in such a familiar spot. He knew Izzy would always be his best friend, but branching out felt pretty good too. Plus, getting to teach them to surf was really exciting. He realized that the only thing better than having a passion was getting to share it.

As Winnie stared across the ocean, she squinted her eyes, wishing she could see just one speck of her parents. She felt bittersweet. She missed her mom and dad very much, but she was also so happy to be sharing this moment with friends. With the sun setting at her back and her friends beside her, she felt the furthest thing from lonely. She smiled knowing that everything was going to be okay.

The four friends looked to each other with a nod of encouragement as, all at once, they took off running toward the ocean. There was nothing but hope ahead of them, as any fears they had were left behind on the shore. Wilder was right. They fell. But they got back up again. And each time they looked around, they were met with the loving smiles of their new friends.

A few short miles away, there was no one left at the school. The bright yellow buses were empty (aside from a few leftover wrappers), and the halls stood perfectly still and silent. Even the teachers were already home, sharing the stories of their first day and planning for the next.

As the sunlight cast one last golden glow throughout the town, a colorful, heart-shaped stepping stone sparkled and beamed behind Sunshine Elementary.

Reader Reviews

"*Sunshine Elementary* is a really good book, definitely one of my favorite books I've ever read. It teaches you life lessons, it's easy to follow, it's well written, and it delivers a positive message. You feel good when you read *Sunshine Elementary*!" **Avery, Age 10**

"I loved how the characters communicated nicely with each other. I can't wait to read the next book!" **Luke, Age 8**

"This book made me feel good inside." **Layla, Age 6**

"I loved the characters because they made so many friends. When Vida was sitting alone and Hanny sat down with her was my favorite part." **Kyle, Age 7**

"I really liked reading this book because it made me feel calm and relaxed. It was a lot more positive than other books and was a fun, easy read." **Max, Age 12**

"I love *Sunshine Elementary* so much that I just want to read it every day!" **Willa, Age 7**

"I love how Hanny helped Vida by being a kind friend. I can't wait for the next book. I'm so excited to find out more!" **Viktor, Age 8**

"I really love the characters, they remind me of me and my friends! They all work together and are actually nice to each other!" **Everly, Age 9**

"I loved the book. I can't wait to know more about all the characters! I really want to read the second book. The first one was so exciting!" **Charlotte, Age 8**

"*Sunshine Elementary* is filled with friendship, laughter, and excitement. The characters are so pure and the ending was spectacular! I can't wait to read the next book!" **Nico, Age 7**

"I loved the whole book! I thought it was so creative, cool, funny, happy and amazing. It gives a better perspective on a kid's life than other books. The characters were funny and good people!" **Meyer, Age 11**

"I liked how all the characters treated each other nicely and were kind. I can't wait to find out more about Lee!" **Isabelle, Age 7**

"I loved how specific the writing was. I want to pretend that I am Hanny. I am so impressed." **Noelle, Age 9**

"I love this book so much because it's nice, awesome, supportive, and kind." **Ollie, Age 5**

"I thought this book was awesome. Kids are usually mean to their parents in books, but this one was unique, nice, cool, funny, and inspiring. A must read. It's a great book!" **Julian, Age 10**

"I loved loved loved it! I think it's the best book ever. Hanny is an engineer and so kind, just like me! It's happy, kind, funny, and friendly." **Audrey, Age 8**

"*Sunshine Elementary* is a unique, captivating, and lifelike story, definitely a must read. I feel as if any age could enjoy this book! If you enjoy entertaining, funny, and inspiring chapter books, this one's for you. Nina has succeeded in weaving so much creativity and positivity in a story so beautiful and full of love. Once you've started, it's hard to put down." **Ava, Age 13**

"I loved that the characters were creative, smart, and curious!" **Chloe, Age 7**

"My students loved *Sunshine Elementary*! They were so excited to hear the next chapter each day and were completely engaged. I love how relatable and diverse the characters are and how unique their families are too. My students were able to connect with the characters easily as they experience events many of my kiddos have also been through. Some have even made comments about wishing they had a friend like Hanny! The overarching theme of kindness is evident and inspiring. We are so excited for the rest of the series!" **Mrs. Wagner, 3rd grade teacher**

About the Author

What Nina Saporta loves more than anything is getting to help make people's lives better. With punk rock roots, a kind heart, and progressive soul, Nina believes that we all have it in us to change the world by leading with kindness. Though she has been writing books for her three children since they were born, *Sunshine Elementary* is the first one she's written to share with the world. Nina lives with her family by the beach in New Jersey. Learn more at www.NinaSaporta.com.

I would like to thank my kids and their magical school for the inspiration; my husband, Ricky, for his certainty; and my family, friends, reviewers, and Kickstarter backers for the love and support. Special thanks to Barbara and James Fetherston, and Mike McLaughlin. Last but not least, infinite gratitude to my amazing editor, Linda Gallant, the Mascot team, and talented illustrators, Amanda Gallant and Chelsea Ekberg, for helping to bring this book to life.

You are *amazing*.